The
Chipmunk King

The Wish Fish Early Reader Series

by Heléna Macalino
Illustrated by: Milena Radeva

Book 2

For: Hally

Helena ♡

CRYSTAL MOSAIC BOOKS

THE CHIPMUNK KING

Text and layout by Heléna Macalino

Copyright© 2016

Illustrated by Milena Radeva

This book is dedicated to Rose, my kitten,
the cuddliest, silliest furball in the world!

Get your free WISH FISH activity book
prepared especially for you by Heléna and Milena!
Go to www.macalino.com

Come little children, I am the Wish Fish and I have a story to tell!

In the shadiest wood near the grassiest hills, in the comfiest tree hole near the sparkliest stream lived a chipmunk. This chipmunk had stripes as sleek as a salmon racing through the river, a tail as puffy as the tall grass gone to seed, and eyes as shiny as the blackberries.

His name was Chippy. Chippy was always at his neighbor Sue's service whenever she needed a hand. He gladly helped her gather seeds when her old legs were too tired to walk.

Chippy had a wonderful life. Except for one thing...

No one ever listened to him.

And he didn't like that at all.

One day, Chippy went camping with his friends. Squeak the Mouse made pine needle tea; Breeze the Blue Magpie swooped from tree to tree gathering more twigs for the fire; while Hopper the Bunny did the most important job of all: she set up the tent for all to sleep in.

Chippy joined Squeak by the fire.

"You have to put in the water before the pine needles, silly," Chippy said.

Squeak stirred the pine needles with a debarked twig. "Well, I always put the pine needles in first to heat them up so they will give more flavor to the water when they are stirred together."

Chippy crossed his arms and rolled his eyes. Then he walked away.

"Nobody listens to me."

"I'm going to go on patrol and to see if Mr. Fox is trying to sneak up on us again," Chippy said.

Chippy climbed the ridgy bark of the nearest oak to get a better view of the forest. Bounding along the rough wood, he sprang to the next branch on a pine tree which barely shook as he landed amongst the smooth, pokey needles. Chippy spotted a brown furry lump next to a sapling by the tiny stream.

Chippy froze; his eyes widened.

"It's a bear!"

Scrabbling so fast he practically flew, Chippy dashed down the tree and over to the campfire.

"There's a bear!" he yelled.

Squeak turned around.

"How could there be a bear? I checked twice, and I didn't see anything. Not a scratch to be seen. Not a paw print to be found."

Chippy growled furiously. "Why doesn't anybody ever listen to me?!"

Hopper hopped over. "Sad to say, you are a little bossy and—"

"RAAARRR!"

"Oh, no! Chippy wasn't just trying to be a know-it-all! Run for your lives!" Breeze shouted.

Chippy ran up the skinny trunk of a young birch tree. Hopper, Squeak, and Breeze scattered in different directions, disappearing into the thick green forest.

The bear sprang into the campsite, swatting over the pot of tea. She let out a rather awkward roar of pain. Chippy gripped his tree branch even harder. He realized he was not that far above the furious bear.

The bear spun around, her burnt paw curled to her chest in pain. Her side slammed into a birch tree, the birch tree Chippy hid on.

Chippy squeaked in surprise as the tree wobbled wildly.

The bear looked up to where Chippy hung onto a branch near the top.

All of a sudden, a familiar bird swooped in.

It was Breeze!

"I'll save you!" she shouted.

"**J**ump onto my back! Quick!" Breeze yelled as she dodged the bear swipes, left and right.

Chippy's fur stood on end; his little tail puffed up; and his claws sunk deep into the bark of the tree as he was holding on for dear life. This was the end!

"Just jump! It's your only chance!" Breeze hollered.

"No! You're insane! I'll never make that jump!" Chippy hollered back.

"You were born to jump. You can do it! NOW JUMP!"

Right then, the bear growled and leaped at Chippy's tree.

Chippy jumped.

The wind fluttered through Chippy's fur as he left the branch. He saw Breeze for a moment beneath him.

Then Breeze was gone.

Chippy fell.

And fell.

And fell.

Then suddenly Chippy felt something feathery and smooth under his tummy. It was Breeze!

Breeze carried Chippy away into the safety of the tall, tall trees where no bear could reach them.

C hippy clung to Breeze and closed his eyes for a moment, I can't believe I just survived that! Chippy opened his eyes and saw all his friends gathered on a tall rock, overlooking their campground.

Breeze landed with a thump next to Hopper and Squeak. Chippy rolled off of Breeze's back, tired and terrified. Down below, Chippy could see the bear completely destroying the campsite in rage over her lost prey.

"Well, by the looks of it, I guess we won't be camping today," Chippy said.

But to himself, he thought: If only they had listened to me, none of this would ever have happened!

Why does nobody ever listen to me?

After they were sure that the bear had gone, the four friends snuck down to the campsite to gather their things. When they had packed away the tea pot—the last of their equipment—they all headed off back into the forest.

Hopper, Breeze, and Squeak talked together about how scary the day had been.

Nobody noticed Chippy walking sad, scared, and alone.

Chippy reached the gate at the base of his great oak tree. Slowly, he climbed the spiral staircase carved into the hollow tree, and went into his house. He dumped his camping tent, his sleeping bag, and his pouch of acorns on the floor next to the window.

Chippy crashed into his nest.

"I wish that everybody would listen to me. Someday one of my friends is going to get hurt."

Burrowing deep into his nest, Chippy slowly fell asleep.

Chippy woke up to the bright morning light shining on his face. He pushed aside some dried grass, then crawled out of his comfy nest. Yawning, he walked over to his cupboard and pulled out a couple of acorns and some pine nut milk. He poured a cup of milk and dropped the acorns into it.

He sat down at his table. Looking out the window, he saw the Chipmunk Fairy's house in the pine tree across the little meadow.

"I remember a couple of months ago the Chipmunk Fairy gave Sue really good advice about medicine for her achy paws."

Leaving behind his breakfast, Chippy got up from his table, ran all the way down his spiral staircase, and across to the Chipmunk Fairy's house.

Chippy knocked on the door excitedly. A voice said, "Come in!"

Inside, the Chipmunk Fairy looked over from feeding her miniature bunny. Her dress had a big fluffy skirt made of rose petals and a top made of leaves. A big white daisy decorated the front. Her slippers were made of seed pods with blades of grass as straps. Her wings fluttered like a busy dragonfly.

"Lately nobody has been listening to me and my friends have been getting into trouble. I'm afraid that someday one of them is going to get very hurt," Chippy said.

The Chipmunk Fairy placed her bunny in its cage and closed the door. "Well, if you are looking for a wish, then you need the Wish Fish.

To seek her out: Find the stream with the sparkliest water. Follow it down to the tree with the mossiest trunk. There she will be waiting."

Chippy ran over dirt and leaves, positive that he knew the right place. He spotted a mossy tree in the distance with a sparkle of blue behind it. But when he got closer, he realized the "stream" was just a patch of blue bells, and the mossy tree was just an old abandoned tree home.

Still determined to find the Wish Fish, Chippy ran on.

But then Chippy spotted a familiar mouse. It was Squeak. Squeak knew where the Wish Fish lived. She'd been there before when she'd wished to become the Mouse Bird.

"Squeak!" Chippy shouted. "Where did you find the Wish Fish?"

"I found her by Breeze's nest out in the North Woods. But wait! Before you go: What wish are you going to make? Remember what happened last time. Always be careful what you wish for!"

"I know! Don't worry about me. I'll be fine!" Chippy shouted as he scurried off.

hippy was out of breath by the time he reached Breeze's nest. From there he could see a very mossy tree. But just being out of breath wouldn't stop Chippy from making his wish come true. He ran to the mossy tree.

There he saw a sparkly stream below, but he looked in it and there was nothing there.

"Hello?" Chippy called out.

"Well, hi there! Are you looking for me?" asked a voice from the water.

Chippy jumped back in surprise. "Are you the Wish Fish?" he asked.

"Yes, I am! Now do you have a wish or are you just saying hi?" the Wish Fish bubbled.

"Of course I have a wish! I wish that everybody would listen to me. They never do!" The Wish Fish jumped out of the water, flipped her fins, and flapped her tail happily. The Wish Fish had gold and silver and blue scales. Her eyes shone blue as the sparkling water, and her tail held the colors of the rainbow.

"Very well then. Stand still or it might go wrong! Golden scale, silver scale, and blue. Combine your power and make my friend's wish come true!"

Poof!
A shower of gold, silver, and blue mist fell away.

In the center now, stood not simply a chipmunk, but the Chipmunk King! Chippy stood taller, his shiny blackberry eyes had a more serious look now like obsidian stones, his grass-gone-to-seed tail stood straight and still.

Even though his sleek stripes had stayed the same, something had changed inside him completely.

"Thank you so very much, Wish Fish. I could never thank you enough," he said. Chippy confidently walked back into the forest.

That night, Chippy stared out the window from his sofa. It was a beautiful night. A perfect night to take a walk under the full moon and the glittering stars. Chippy got up from his sofa and scampered to Squeak's house. Because Squeak was coming with him.

When Chippy got to Squeak's door decorated with pine cones, swirls, and trees, he stood on her tidy welcome mat and knocked. A couple seconds later, Squeak answered. Squeak wore a nightcap and a pair of pink slippers.

"What do you need at this late hour?" she asked sleepily.

"I want you to go on a walk with me in the night right now," the Chipmunk King commanded.

Squeak gulped. "Chippy, you know how scared I am of the dark. Can we please go in the daytime another day?"

"NO."

Chippy saw Squeak stiffen and say in a frightened voice, "Okay, I will go."

Yes! It's working. My wish actually came true. The Squeak I know would never in her life say yes to this, Chippy thought.

A moment later, Squeak was back without her sleeping cap and pink slippers.

"Let's go!" said Chippy.

"O-oo-kay," Squeak replied and followed Chippy out into the deep dark forest.

As they walked, they passed by Hopper's burrow. Chippy heard Hopper rustling and bustling inside. Hopper's head popped out of her little hole.

"What are you doing out in the middle of the night with - Squeak?! I thought you hated the dark, Squeak?" Hopper asked.

Squeak did not say anything.

"Come on, Squeak, let's go," said Chippy.

As soon as Chippy and Squeak started to walk away, Chippy heard fast thumping, headed north. Hopper was getting Breeze, he realized. A moment later, Hopper and Breeze appeared next to Squeak.

"What are you doing, Chippy?" Breeze asked. "Are you okay? I know you would never do this to Squeak. Let her go home. We should all go home. Even—"

"NO!" Chippy yelled.

Then Hopper and Breeze stiffened and replied, "Okay." Just like Squeak did.

The four friends walked through the plants of the forest floor—over the moss, around the mushrooms, and through the ferns. Chippy felt the spongey moss on his little paws; he felt the shakes run down from his heart to his little knees. He looked to both sides of himself. He saw all of his friends' faces. They all had frowns and Squeak was trembling.

All of them were miserable - even Chippy.

And then Chippy heard a twig snap.

"The bear is back!" yelled Squeak. "Everybody run!"

"No!" bellowed the Chipmunk King. "I give the commands around here and you will listen!"

All three of Chippy's friends stiffened and said, "Okay."

"See that den over there? It looks abandoned. Let's go hide in there. The bear will never find us."

Chippy led them into the den. Inside the den, something fluffy got stuck between his toes. He plucked it out. It was bear fur! This was the bear's den!

"The bear's coming!" cried Breeze. "What do we do, Chippy?!"

Chippy shook. He realized his horrible mistake. "I don't know. I should never have made that wish! I thought I would know everything. But no one is always right. Can you guys please help me?"

"I know what to do!" Hopper said.

Hopper and Squeak dove straight to work burrowing into the wall. Chippy heard the fast thumping of the bear's paws coming nearer and nearer. Dirt flew everywhere. Chippy and Breeze sheltered each other from the soil and rocks.

"The tunnel out is done! Let's go!" Squeak squeaked.

The four friends dove through the tunnel just as the bear pounced. She was far too big to get through. They were saved!

Even though it was the middle of the night, Chippy bolted straight for the North Woods and the Wish Fish. When Chippy arrived at the sparkliest stream, the Wish Fish was already waiting.

"Oh, Wish Fish! I came to tell you that I've learned my lesson. Nobody knows everything all the time!"

The Wish Fish said, "I am so happy you learned your lesson, my friend. Now let's get your wish reversed. Remember, stand still or it might go wrong! Golden scale, silver scale, and blue. Combine your power and make my friend's wish come true!"

Poof!
A shower of gold, silver, and blue mist fell away.

In the center now stood a beautiful chipmunk. This chipmunk had stripes as sleek as a salmon racing through the river, a tail as puffy as the tall grass gone to seed, and eyes as shiny as the blackberries.

Now instead of a proud and bossy chipmunk, stood a good friend.

"Thank you so much. I will always remember you for this!" he said and scampered off into the night and back home.

The next afternoon the four friends met at Chippy's house for a tea party. Chippy set out tiny pine nut biscuits, hibiscus-acorn tea, and seed scones. Once everyone had arrived, Chippy apologized to them for his bossiness and to his surprise, they apologized to him for not listening. They raised their tea cups to forever friendship.

Chippy smiled. Chippy had a wonderful life. Especially one thing...

He listened to his friends, and they listened to him.

(At least, most of the time!)

And he liked that most of all.

ABOUT THE AUTHOR

Heléna Macalino loves to explore her dreams. She wanders along lovely garden paths with magical gates, finds her way into enchanted forests with animals who hide huge wishes in their hearts. And as a member of a family of writers, she records these adventures to share with fellow wanderers. Heléna wrote her first book when she was in 2nd grade, THE REFLECTION, an Alice in Wonderland-style picture book about a little girl who falls through the reflection of a puddle. Now a 4th grader, Heléna brings you her third book, THE CHIPMUNK KING from her series THE WISH FISH.

Want to follow Heléna and her new bunny in her wanderings? When she's not cuddling with her cats or doodling in her drawing notebook, she can be found on her family's website:

www.macalino.com

Subscribe to her newsletter on the website and be the first to know when the next edition of THE WISH FISH appears!

ABOUT THE ILLUSTRATOR

Milena Radeva is a dream-maker. She loves the magic of colours and their power to turn imagination into reality. Reality which every one of us can see, touch and feel in her children's books illustrations. Milena started drawing professionally when she was 12 years old, she studied in an Art high school, she has BA and MA in illustration and now she is working on her PhD. She has illustrated many children's books for authors from all around the world, and she is always looking for new book adventures, magical stories and cheerful characters. Because for her, every new book is a whole new world to be discovered.

If you are interested in Milena's artworks you can dive in her drawings by following her on facebook – MilenaRadevaArts or visit her website:

www.milena.seimenus.com

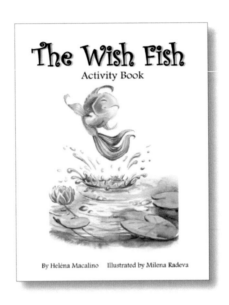

The Wish Fish
Activity Book

By Heléna Macalino   Illustrated by Milena Radeva

Get your free WISH FISH activity book
prepared especially for you by Heléna and Milena!
Go to www.macalino.com

COMING SOON

The third book in the WISH FISH SERIES:
THE WINTER MAGPIE

Wishes can be made in the woods!

Breeze the Blue Magpie has a wonderful life, playing in the fluffy leaves in the fall.

One afternoon, a terrible winter blizzard strikes! Breeze finally gives up playing, only to find her nest destroyed and all of the food buried under the icy snow. A frozen, lost little Breeze doesn't realize that getting ready for winter first would let her enjoy herself and her friends Squeak, Chippy, and Hopper all winter long.

Then she meets the Wish Fish...

Be careful what you wish for!

Made in the USA
Middletown, DE
16 July 2019